STARLESSNESS

graham wells

Red Shoes

RED SHOES

Published by *Red Shoes*
Red Shoes, 20 Queensway North, Walton-on-Thames, Surrey, KT12 5QW

starlessness first published in England by Red Shoes 1995
Written by graham wells 2nd Dec 1994 and 21st Feb 1995
1 3 5 7 9 10 8 6 4 2

A CIP record for this title
is available from the British Library

ISBN 0 9526431 0 3

Printed in England by Biddles
Set in Poliphilus

ABOUT JAMES

ABOUT JAMES

ONE

WHEN last I saw James he was pretty sick, most close to dying. On those few days his very way of living really had become unmanageable, and the tale which he told me caused me the gravest distress. It was a desperate, comfortless tale, truly sorrowful, that his vanishing as he did when so thoroughly ill, still now worries me with the fate with which he may have befallen.

For a while my friend was failing badly in his work at the university laboratory, most always was he absent. Until then he was doing very well, at twenty-seven it had all fallen away. His dietary habits were particularly deviant, so much had they interfered with his academic ability. They were most unpleasant. Only would he ever eat raw fish. He was most strict about this, and only ate once a day. So a extreme diet quite simply is unable to sustain life for very long. James was starving himself; and he was going to die. It *was* this serious.

How all this came to be, I don't truly know. James was a keen neurobiologist. When students I remember how he use to always be in awe of invertebrates and how their nervous systems be so amenable to cellular studies. With sparkle he would tell me the neurobiological advantages of studying marine molluscs and crustacea, and how they have far fewer nerve cells than mammalian brains and so their nervous systems may be easily mapped, and how too because invertebrate neurones are extremely large, each individual cell and its connections may be readily identified and each cell numbered. The beauty really was, he would tell me, the colossal sizing of these nerve cells, for this so makes open the detailed analysis of nerve cells, either singly or in combination, to using microelectrodes, the electron microscope and biochemical techniques. He truly did find these marine beasts quite wonderful.

So to have hear of all this came to me a terrible surprise. Pure sciences, and too fine arts and philosophy, he really did see to be absolutely invaluable. Though a scientist himself, he was not the kind who exaggerated the attainments of science and made little of those of art. He was very much the opposite, and once had a bitter argument with a fellow physiology student who supposed the studies of classics and Egyptology to be far less demanding than that of biology. To James, so a view was simply a wrongful impression to have, and too most damaging. With curtail on university education, so a partiality is only helpful in the reducing of academic excellence, would he say. So a opinionated reasoning only ever causes particle physics and chemical engineering to be the only schools in receipt of any sensible finance; and even then, one of them would have to go. The worth of all pure researches and academic freedom, in his eyes, really was above price; and a view as this, so opposed to the very way of the world, I feel may in some way have been part of the problem.

And the way of the world to me does seem

important. Very much did the way of the world imperil my friend's life. As is made most clear by those thin finances afforded to our research councils, those at Westminster earnestly believe true science and art be thoroughly useless. This must be so, for they simply give away university laboratories to pharmacy and biotechnology syndicators; and this be most cynical to the truth of how everything applied and commercial owes all to the pure researches which be living soul of a university. A retail mentality wants only to take away academic freedom and kill all creative thinking. Without freedom natural sciences and pure researches simply are without chance. This is the way of the world, and when seeing all that passes for science is to be the dictate of retailers, in so a world my friend was just unable to thrive.

Though I myself know precious little neurobiology, I know James had been doing worthwhile research. This must surely have been so, for his work was so integral to the proposal on the professor's grant application. My friend had at least finished the data analysis from his last experiments before falling too ill, though a manuscript suitable for publication had not been forthcoming. To the professor this too was concern. Seeking the renewal of this vital research grant for the laboratory he had been most patient waiting on this paper. With monies for medical research only being made available upon the number of articles appearing in the premier journals he did so badly need this paper to make safe the award. This is the criterion by which scientific progress is measured, and Dr James Gray with his life in disrepair and fading, was incapable to anymore.

When having received the professor's phone call I was positively and most deeply shocked. I was finishing breakfast and making ready for work. With little time to explain he was necessarily brief saying only that the inveterate anorexia which tormented James was now an immediate threat to his life. A particular hurt too was delivered by this displeasing conversation, together with this feeling of deep shock, for I had not seen James for some eighteen months, and all the wishful undoing which hindsight brings to a conscience full with regret started hereafter. Believing me to be James's closest friend, the professor urged I postpone everything and meet him in Russell Square.

Naturally I at once left my Barnsbury flat, jumped straight on a 14 bus, and stood dependent, with hurry in my mind through the jam to Euston. Running down Woburn Place I leaped the traffic lights at Tavistock Square and arrived to find the professor already waiting. He was with two psychiatrists and James's GP. There in the heat of a June morning sun I received account of the whole affair. The situation was severe; James weighed not seven stone, and it was imperative he start eating. Listening to trained explanation I was quite open to persuasion, and readily compliant with their knowledgeable solution. I thus agreed to take them up to my friend's attic dwellings, which were housed on a sidestreet a little way off from the square.

As we ascended the stairwell of the rundown Georgian house, very much did I have second thoughts about my part in all this; for I was the good friend who would make him 'see reason'. What kind of option did he really have? Either way he was to be hospitalized. We *were* going to have him sectioned. When we reached the top, I was sickened in my own reproach.

The door was left ajar, the keys too just hanging in the lock. I turned to the others as if needing consent from formal and certain expressions before proceeding further. With their looks of reassuring approval I lead them into the small apartment, still feeling this was very wrong. The professor was close behind, he went one way and I straight into the kitchen. The clinicians, creating space, waited quietly in the doorway. I ran to the window, looked out at nothing in case of sounds from other rooms. All was quiet, James had gone. Thankful, I opened the window, turned and leaned back on the kitchen sink.

The place was so clean and Spartan with everything put away, apart from a dinner which was left uneaten. Cutlery and an uncooked salmon steak were lay set on a blue china plate where James would sit at the end of the table. The fish was untouched, and the cafetiere which stood there also was still a little warm and this I would keep quiet.

I then went to join the professor in the study. He was politely nosing among the bookshelves, perhaps hoping to have see of some workings of a manuscript. The professor was quite respectful about this really, he would never infringe contents of desk drawers and filing cabinets no matter his need. The professor looked at me and the clinicians came into the study, there was nothing to be done, James really had vanished. Some compact and serious discussion followed and then it was over, the professor had to travel to Oxford to give an afternoon seminar and the medics too had important appointments to meet. When conversing on the thorough sadness of it all the professor thanked me and I agreed to take care of things and lock up, and this I was very glad to do. It was an unhappy morning, and they then made well their leave.

TWO

ALONE in his study the day so far had jarred my senses. My friend was in a mess, he had thrown away everything. James's cherished copy of *Nerve, Muscle, and Synapse* was left discarded on the sofa. It was laying next to a novel about romance, the writing of his favourite German author. I picked up the little textbook which I knew had made a great impression even then way back when we first had met. I so wanted to help him now; there was just nothing I could do.

The room was filled with books and journals and things, the best love he ever had. All over, countless books were shelved free from order, without any formal arranging. Many homeless titles too made simple stacks wherever there would be empty wall space. There were no other possessions of any remark, only an old wireless and a small number of plants. Otherwise, he was of very few belongings.

I looked at the titles before me. The line started with Kuffler and Nicholls, an IBRO handbook in immunohistochemistry, and a sizeable cell biology text; all as perhaps would be expected. Then there stood, *The Treasure of the Sierra Madre*, an autobiography by Otto Frisch, *The Observer's Book of Wild Animals of the British Isles*, and an old school-book on mathematics. Mathematics was not my friend's forte, and he really saw this as a huge personal failing. Neither was he disastrously bad, he only wanted more feeling for a subject he believed to be fine art. He cared about history though, and this helped him have appreciation of the art; I remember once how he became intrigued by Godel's Incompleteness Theorem and started reading, 'On Formally Undecidable Propositions...'. He would try and imagine the electrifying effect of Proposition VI on adherents to *Principia Mathematica*; in 1931 it must have been thoroughly disorienting. I was sure somewhere he must still have in his keep translation of this paper he once tried so hard to understand.

It was only with my browsing along the shelves that I came to discover my friend's doctoral treatise. It was bound in Prussian blue, with gold lettering along the spine which read, *'Ph.D. 1987 J. Gray'*. These experimental studies were in the neurobiology of the opisthobranch mollusc *Aplysia californica*, a herbivorous marine snail which feeds on seaweed. To me they were quite an achievement; having completed these careful researches within the three years James was still only twenty-four when he received his Ph.D. I pulled down the volume and went to sit down at my friend's desk.

I turned through the pages; the thesis was replete with clear delineated figures of intracellular recordings, high magnification electron micrographs of synaptic boutons, and too the most colourful photomicrographs of cells under the light microscope stained with intense neuroanatomical markers in differing hues. Were there too, detailed camera lucida drawings of *Aplysia* nervous system, and diagrams of the experimental apparatus and electrical circuits, and many, many, of those complex equations frequently used in neurophysiology.

As a student I read anthropology, and started undergraduate life with an innocent notion that sciences were simply about hypotheses testing, as if they were only being straight forward empiricism and nothing else. It is not as so, science is far more than that, it too is art. Looking through these pages, James had clearly been afforded with uncommon ability, a truly effectual ability which set him apart from most others. Too is it one I fall short of and am able only to specify in terms of an ingenuous admiration. James possessed a scientist brain, having every necessary aptitude and intellect which scientists most surely do have. I say this very much the same way as a great composer indeed must have a music brain, though I am wholly unable to read music. And these pages to me, were like sheets of music. Inelegant description I know, and on my friend's capability, to remark further, only would be more so.

That I am not an academic is quite unhidden then, and so do know not anything on the workings of scientists' minds. Though on what motivated James I do know a little of. He did only have one true desire; a real hunger for knowledge. James distinctly had a genuine need to seek understanding of nature. And this hunger, which he did so have, I do firmly believe be authentic in some people.

I was about to reshelve my friend's work when I noticed the honeybee project. It was behind glass on the bottom shelf of the bookcase, just to the side of me, down by my feet. I recognized it at once, it had one of those black plastic ring spines which all students use to bind their final year B.Sc. projects. I opened the bookcase and picked up the project. It had that dusty paper feel about it, which you too could taste in your mouth when turning over the pages. The study looked plain by comparison; just simple description of honeybee visual system. It was quite innocent really, and had its gleaming typing errors and foggy photographs just as most undergraduate projects do.

Notably, it was this modest honeybee dissertation which made me realize how young my friend really was, and with having that unaffected ardour. Though he was very inspirited, in no meaning was it in anyway too assuming. He was not of the kind who went into research with a benefit for mankind value; and neither had he wish to assert any personalized interpretation of the universe over any other. It was only that he possessed all that feeling of purpose and intent which people do have when they are that young. James did just love doing science.

When having closed these loosely bound leaves did it dawn on me how I knew nothing whatsoever on the nature of his post-doctoral studies. Though way before then, when James started on his postgraduate training, I decided to make my livelihood out of writing software; first out in Berkshire where I met Claudine, and then in the City; it was at about the right time. We remained close friends throughout, I guess I just lost that fascination for everything philosophical which he of course retained. Very much was James a giving person, and with all the interest he showed in matters new to my life was he most acceptable to change; and in friendship did he too see that change need not always make distance. That was the failing in me. So it soon came to be we rarely ever discussed scientific issues to any detail. All to my shame then, on my friend's most recent studies, I really do have no remark.

There were no signs to give away. On his desk only was there one last treasure left outcast; *The Anatomy of the Common Squid Loligo peallii Lesueur*, by L.W. Williams. That it was in the actual nature of his very last researches which was causing my friend be so upset was to me then only simple conjecture. With guilty feeling and my reflectiveness I soon thought about starting for work. For sure work was flexible enough for me to be late once in a while but this morning I had not even phoned in, and practicalities hanging over me and responsibility to my own living were only adding to my self-accusation. Have I too, required accountability to an overseer.

I got up and walked over to the skylight as if the sun and heatwave were going to improve the situation. There were no curtains and white gloss paint with city dirt was peeling from the wooden panes, and there in the sunshine on the window sill all this time had sat the letter. Set vertical to the glass and being held by my friend's harmonica, was it left in quite plain aspect. So preoccupied had been the professor when looking for the manuscript that he missed to see this ordinary and manila envelope. There was no address, and neither was it sealed. Impatiently I opened up the letter. The scrawl to me was at once recognizable and read as follows.

To whoever,

I know that I am completely and utterly insane. When I look at the world all around, what passes for sanity I completely fail to understand. In so a world which just be hateful, further seeking in scientific explanation to me only do seem be a absolute madness.

So long.

James.

This plain little letter read so unalike him; and too was it hurtful. That these only few lines were so thin, unfinished, was simply furthermore say of how he had discarded all he had ever known. In the gaunt italic script and black ink were his sadness and despair so showing.

I made two folds in my friend's words and placed them deep into the pocket inside of my blazer. The toy harmonica on the window sill too was a sign to me. It really was the kind a child would wake up and find in his Christmas stocking, and too had his grandfather given it just as so when James was very young. Assuredly, I knew then where James would be. All the same, I still made ready for work.

Whether it was the strain or me just being self-interested which made me behave in this way I am uncertain. Only, if it were the other way, and it had been me who was in need, James would have been there for sure. When leaving his deserted dwellings I took my friend's harmonica and placed it somewhere in the shade. Maybe it was me who had changed, not James.

THREE

When the Saturday arrived I went in search of James. From on top of the Victorian lock and weir bridge I looked out on the village downstream where I hoped he would be. High above the river the climate seemed far less sultry than down on the ground and the warm breeze all around too was fresh by any contrast. The previous day, as was the day before so very sad, also had been one clouded, with reminiscings of my friend subduing all thoughts of other kind, and so I was contented to be away from the city. Though not too far from town, just a little west on the District Line, I was stood before this remote and wonderful, and extraordinarily green, settlement.

The sun ablaze in the sky over my shoulders, evaporated haze off the river in front of the village shoreline, and a thickly wooded ait took centrestage of the view. Afore the island an array of houseboats were moored against the north bank, and inland of these could I see the row of terraced houses where James's grandfather had lived all his life, and where also James had been born. Beyond the terrace were the towers and rooftops of the old square too partly visible where on occasion they breached the vast leafy bows which were a cloak around the village. Along the bank a little further still, could I also see just a small stretch of the promenade where it became unhidden from behind the ait. The village possessed a peacefulness, and it was here by the river where my friend would be most every weekend.

Having tarried too long on the footbridge I restarted on my way towards the steps at the end. Taking one last look at the skyline I made my descent.

When walking along the tow-path I was reminded of the gas bill. It was purely because I gave promise to Claudine the charge would be settled that very morning that it did so come to mind. Too often had so a concern for domesticities filled times which would have otherwise been better shared with a friend. Do not think my life with Claudine is anything less than perfectly happy, I am very much in love. On no account is she in anyway to blame for my failing. To the contrary, she really was quite taken with James, always had she made him welcome in our home. Distant in recriminations did the bill seem so unimportant then. Twice forgotten and still owed was it passive inside my jacket.

All at once were these repentant feelings disturbed when a child's voice called out at me.

'Hey, Mister!'

The cry came from beneath my feet, and I looked down to see a boy of about nine clamber up from the water's edge.

'Hey, Mister,' he said again exhausted when reaching the top, 'you wanna buy some eels off me?'

There was a young girl with him, she was standing with a fishing rod by a very large bucket, and I could see the snakelike fish writhe inside.

'Don't like em,' I said wholly free of untruth.

'Ol! Go on Mister,' he pleaded.

I gave him two pound coins and told him how he was to stew the catch and have with mashed potato, which he of course already knew.

'Cor! Thanks Mister,' he cheered, and ran off quickly, jumping back down the riverbank to rejoin his friend.

The afternoon was moving by me so I lengthened step a little and let the children to their fishing. The tow-path soon left the river to come out on a sheltered, twisting road. To the right was there a small humpback bridge which I crossed over to follow the winding until I came upon the terrace.

The row reached so very far. The houses were quiet and the street was lazy. There was a black dog barking, and all the time was I thinking, what was I really to expect? I had resisted to first phone for care my friend, leaving as he did before, would do so again. Then there was the kindly old man, James's grandfather, whom I had met on only a few occasions. Too was I uncertain of the opinion he would have of the kind of friend I really was. With no expectation did I soon arrive outside the house.

Though James's grandfather was once himself a gardener his was a very simple one, with only a cared for lawn and a modest rose growing to the distant side of the front window. James spoke often and well of his grandfather who once tended to the magnificent gardens of the crown property close by, and too the wooded landscape in a nearby Royal Park. As were all the other doors along the terrace, so his front door too was painted navy blue. The black dog in the middle of the road watched me soundlessly at the garden gate. I walked up to the house and knocked.

The door was soon answered, and when the old man recognized me, at once was I made at ease. With short combed back hair and his friendly looking features, he seemed most unsurprised to see me. 'Hello Paul,' was all he said, 'come on in,' and I followed him through the hallway and into the kitchen. 'Have a seat,' he said, 'and I'll find you a drink.'

There was a chair in the corner embedded between the table and the gas stove, and I sat down while the old man went to the pantry. The evening sun made bright the kitchen so I was sure to notice how like my friend's this room too was so very clean and with modest furnishing. Through the window, amidst the backyards and clothes-lines could I see the disused air raid siren which stood before the second row of houses. The old man brought to the table two bottles of beer, opened one, and handed me a glass. He retired to the armchair opposite me where he was shaded by the side of the window and together we poured our drinks.

That he was a man with sympathy and ruth was revealed in his quietness. Was there very much this gentleness about him, a calmness which was only of his years, and which too was quite unasking. Very much had he this something which made me settle in his company.

'James,' I then asked of him, 'how is he?'

To me he told everything of his poor grandson's starvation, and how he was so very thin. Of how the girl from down the road had discovered him just laying in a cold, cold, sunrise and carried him to the front door. How he was so unwell and most close to dying. Was it only a fortune which had seen him home in this very morning.

When to me all this he had unfolded was I again in shame. With the conversation closed and his compassion told he said for me to see James and showed me to the kitchen door. All by myself in the hall and unable to foresee, I wouldn't think twice on the room at the top of the stairs. When outside on the landing, straight away I knocked, marked time in abeyance, and then walked in.

The bedroom was dark with shade and sundown. Window curtains waved in a evening air, with yellow-orange of a sodium street lamp flare on the wardrobe mirror. Quietly I moved close to where my friend lay. When I looked in his eyes were all the radiant and flame just gone. Was there only left of him in thorough emaciation and impoverished. Were those dark eyes of his so cruelly starved.

Watchful over all that was strung out inside of me I sat down at his side, and though he was so weak and poorly, he begged me listen to his every say. There in words so true I heard his most unhappy tale.

JAMES'S TALE

JAMES'S TALE

ONE

WERE I all used up and ruin, with my only sweet life thrown to the lions. And were the brain a real bastard to me, and had it been that way for very long now. And were it always be that way to me. Though I do treat it kindly. Were I only feed it on a raw fish with a 'essential' amino acids in and Omega-3's. Do it only make me be so thin and waste away when I do be so hungry. And so, behind a blue door, me were not too well again.

Fall over in the kitchen, walls all do move round in a circle, and poor grandpop, he just be down at the pub. He just be stranded there. And the lonely note on the table do tell me that. Must I leave him a message, and say how I do be at home and all safely lock away in a darkened room. With my only town keys so leave alone in a apartment front door do I just abandon everything I have ever known. And do I just be prodigal that way, poor grandpop do know that. Were he going to kill that fat calf in the backyard.

Were things very bad though, and me, were me unable to write anymore. Have a handwriting ataxia impair me so. And have the brain done this to me. Take away a motor skill and not have fingers do a cursive script anymore with legible letters forming in it, and me were only have a dysgraphia now. Though were this no real matter. A aphasia damage the brain too do have. Were the tongue only say; 'banana, armadillo, tap-water, Jupiter,' now. Can only talk babble with a word salad in. Do the constructing of a sentence with linguistic and semantic value just be a airy dream of mine.

And were these symptoms unkind to me every day now, only this morning were no ordinary fuck, it were a real fancy occasion.

With no proprioceptor, and me have no sense of kinaesthesia, were my bony claw fingers try clench all the money in my jeans' pocket. Very motion amiss and no control it just do fall cascade off of the table, and I do not care and watch it do loops on the lino. But there were sterling and a hundred English pounds all go astray in my get here this morning and I can't account for it. Were a plain arithmetical operation prove too difficult for me. Though a retarding innumeracy do start scarify me a bit. When I can't add up it do put a terror in me. Do make me think I got a brain damage. Do make me think I gone too far. For a peace of mind, I try hard with a seven times table, and I can't do it. I can't! Because I were a horrible mess.

And were I only treading water and be so desperate. And I do have to go to the fridge. Though I not want to do this. Were me have starvely eyes and see me a skipjack tuna tin with a condensation chill on be too mouthwatering and drool; and a only baby brown trout, lightly poach and everything, do want me eat it too. Do the brain mistreat me though. Do it never want me to have food or anything, and be overly cruel that way. With a salivary reflex subdued, and no vagal coordination of gastric HCl with pepsinogen in, and no hopefulness, seem me have no usual digestive responsiveness left anymore. And do the brain only tell me very firmly lies and double-cross me that way, and I were wish all this be unbelievable.

With unkind circles, and a faintliness, sail inhumanely in my eyes were a lose of consciousness coming up and I do understand emergency. Were nerve injury, and hurting, quite imminent and quite promised then. Though I do see the yeast extract, and it were standing so close to the milk. Permanently rich in thiamine, it were have every vitamin in a B complex in it, and it were a only mercy left going to save me have a Wernicke's encephalitis. So when I discover how the tamper proof seal were profanely intruded, well, my heart do simply break. And I were know that panacea have been poisoned now. With acutely toxophobia I do be very aware of these things. And I do be forever in anguishment that way and always have foreboding too. Though everything did be too doubtful now. In that I were mouse-trapped in a capsule with Pandemonium frenzy and red danger, so were I have to have bad medicine.

Wipey, wipey, with a Kleenex and I do go clean the taps and I am only stone crazy. Do it be alarming when wild upset and a fretfulness throw me whirly in a handwashing ritual. Wash, wash, wash, were unending repetition of seemingly senseless behaviour pattern a actual pathology in me, brain do buzz like a bee. But mandatory forces coerce me in infrangible cycles, which be too habitual, and steal away all my sweet time. Were they repress me harshly in frustration, be too unsuccessful for me to break free, only do have me be very tearful.

Teaspoon rinse under running tap I do feel my heart beat. And it were only a witch's potion which make my heart do that. With chlorinating agents and herbicides in and I just be cleansing my cutlery in carcinogen and insecticide. And all along it was the tap-water which was making me ill and I did know that. All along I did know that. And it is people who do this. People make unwell the drinking water. And kill all the fish too!

Thanks to migraine do be truly unforgiving, with deathly teaspoon me were have to have that vitiate thiamine and B complex now, because my dying were so close at hand. Only, my eyes were seeing that murderous cat saucer lay very clean in the corner. So were it a factual certainty me have just ingest a lethal catfood morsel left smudge on a tap spout in a error-ridden saucer wash merely fall down on my little spoon. So I were very rueful and bewail; 'if only I had decontaminated the taps with a Kleenex first.' And were a ensnarement in hygiene ritual and stereotypy always erasing my memory like that, a single scrapie prion going to lay my brain to waste. Just do bad protein synthesis and have neuronal devastation, and I were go to Hell. Owe to there were once a Minister appear on a television screen who did have worldly wisdom and say how meat do be a very safe food and just eat steak tartare. And he do say he going to give his only homeless childs a hamburger to eat as well. And he just be a real bastard to do that.

Worst woe betide me yet though.

All the time were palpitations escalating, and me

do have a dreadful, dreadfulness. Too overly foot down in the heartrate accelerator really do drive the tachycardia too fast, and be so intolerable, noradrenalin do drench my heart. And there were taste in my mouth! There were going to be myocardial unpleasantness, and give me a cardiac arrest. Coronary arteries would be broken and I would bleed my heart out. 'Oh! Please slow my heart down;' with sweet Jesus I do make so a plea. And He just say, 'No!'

Quietly turn away, and leave me feel flames.

Were high-pitch of a very, very, high spatial frequency screech into my hair cells in my organ of Corti. Which do convert terrible sound signal into nerve impulse and damn the rest of me. Din and volume scream along my VIIIth nerve and do ruin ascending tonotopically organized brain structures and wreck my acoustic senses completely! And there were a insufferable toothache developing too, and this were acutely painful. So, deeply drown in a trigeminal neuralgia were my poor head just then go and do. With tensely contracting musculature be very tight round my cranium, under taut mandibles do my clean white teeth just crumble. No more was I able to bear.

Then the migraine were most merciless too! Only weakening meninges with a tear in arachnoid do hold my brain be crush mash against hard bone, were my eyes just be indistinct with watery and blur. Thoroughly immense intracranial pressure do increase inside my skull, were very real evil be hanging over me. Inflammation seethe and swell, just do need a vent, and my head was going to explode. And there was nothing I can do. And it were all be so simple; dura would tear, my skull would fracture, and my brains would fulminate. And I just want to scream!

Terror-strick, for a last chance, insanely me do turn out my jeans' pockets; 'My pillbox! I did still have it!' Very frantic were me, graceless fingers do tangle with the latch — and for ever go by me — and have miracle succeed in me make open the simple conceal. Oh, I do be in a hurry, and sweep down me a only two Valium left in the world.

Sadly it were much too late.

So deep inside my head the sound did come. 'Click'. It were just that. 'Click'. It was a pitiless sound, which seemed to say; 'A most terrible thing is going to happen to you, James, from which you are never, ever, going to recover. Do you an untold harm and be permanently maim.' And then it did befallen me. Middle cerebral artery did bleed all over motor cortex. Just paralyse me completely numb, brain do soak up blood like a sponge. Were it just very corrosive, and bleach, living nervous tissue just do die and be useless.

There was very much trauma. Wholly deaf, a high decibel tinnitus be a only noise to me, and the bloodshed do trickle down from my ear. And were me twitching very badly, and I were quite unable to think. Painstaking and no avail me do collapse at 'D' in my 'ABC', there really was very much trauma, even in counting to ten I were derelict. Were my childhood memories and everything have be removed, did be so sad, nothing faintly cognitive do remain. Very anxious and try, me truly do not be able to think! Were I so froze insensible with amnesia, I not know my own name. So were my unfortunate nervous system wholly ruined and be unreparable and were my life be through. Whereabouts I were only debris.

Thoroughly in depletion, and feel very tired, I were sat at the kitchen table, my little head in my hands and broken-down. And me were unable to satisfy a vague but emphatic urge to weep. And the tremors did prevent me from sitting very still. All the time me do be so extremely jumpy. And me were actually have chorea and a St Vitus' Dance. Though it would go away. I just do have to wait patiently, stare down at that red loafer shoe of mine and wait. Achy body limbs move involuntary movements. Pull on a white cotton sock and wait on a tenterhook.

Eventually were I allowed to stand on my own two feet. Were me wander me over to the cabinet hung above the kitchen sink and take me a good look in the mirror. 'James, is that really you?' Plaintive reflection do not reply. I was a very sorry boy. Tremulous duplicate do be wringing wet, with a fiery pyrexia shiver and coldness perspire. Have me feel of my hair, and kneading my T-shirt, it truly was me. Did the sudor and tremor just elude me when the brain fever were a critical thing and I not be that attentive. I was cold though. And thirsty too. What I really needed was a warm drink. All the same, me were have to lean against that kitchen sink and wait with calm endurance, steady like a leaf, for my streaming clothes were soon be drip-dry and a Valium to hit. When I do become capable of a half-reason were me going to make a hot coffee.

And when the diazepam do work, somehow bind to a regulatory subunit in a GABA receptor and let

33

transmitter interaction with a binding site be very more effective. This overly enhanced uptake of GABA at a post-synaptic receptor site just be very tranquil for the central nervous system and deliver me from evil that way.

'Oh, how joyously normal I again did feel!' Wholly pacific and tender-heart were I like a peaceful dove, and I were a kind person again. And I do be freely capable with attending to my own dehydration need state and be very collected as well. Which let me think a bit better and go to the cupboard and find my friendly cafetiere, which say 'hello' to me. Were my sorely throat parch dry though, and I did think that with this hot coffee to give that manuscript a last look would be a prudent thing to do. A anticipating of a aroma of a freshly roast Java bean grind away in the electric mill were make me go wild for a moment. Alas, me were very disappointed when I do come to open the pantry door. It be so unfulfilling, were I not have any of those coffee beans left anymore. No matter though, would the all-day coffee-house be open in the town square. In my calm composure this kind of thing do occur to me. Were my usual preference to remain asocial not be a obstacle anymore, so were I quite agreeable to take coffee out, — very spontaneous was I these days. And I were in no mad hurry, would the manuscript wait, it were go nowhere and be no emergency for me to read; and bear in mind my semblance, I do think it sane to shower first. Cause me delay with ablutions were only make me yearn, and have longing. Slake my thirst with a warm drink were be more pleasing that way.

Were me only leave me the kitchen with the wondering, 'Would my favourite navy T-shirt match my very blue jeans?' There were no real thoughts to make me worry, I was mindlessly happy! Buoyant like a new born Thoroughbred foal do me leap up them stairs, dreamy for the bathroom and be so carefree. And when the Devil did meet me only a few moments ago, and say how I do be extremely mortal and will one day go to Hell, well, I just do forget about that. Because would me be on the street soon, and run all the way to the coffee-shop.

TWO

WERE the old square be suntrap, and white-hot, in a post-noon time of day. And were it very town-like, and have villagey feel as well, and be very pretty too. And were a sensitivity to beauty and the world with a set of principles of good taste a real concern to me, and were I very sensitive that way, and be aesthetical. Though tunnelly-vision me too do have. And it be true, I were not able to grasp wider implications far away from my central point of view. Me only see cafe-bar parasols make a row at the far end of the square, and be focussed like that. When I do need a coffee.

Go into the coffee-bar have me a corner table, where two walls protect my back, so me can see the world go by in safety. The waitress, she do take my order. They not have no Java. And I not want to worry her. Say Columbian would do so fine. Were I not wanting to be acting foolish like that. And she do go away, and me I wait so patiently with a simple mental activity go on in my head.

Were a warm coffee quite a good thing to have really. Warm flavour just do comfort me. Stop me feel so hungry. Were I wanting to feel happy. Though it were not to be that way. I just see that Miss Kitty Queen-Cake perch up over there on her pedestal. And I know her, she were in my class at school in a bygone yesteryear. And I not want to see her.

And I were quite worried though, if she should see a lonely me, somehow recognize me, what were I to say? With her glamour were she always have her overly playground charisma, and if I say to her about cAMP as a 'second messenger' in the action of adrenalin induced release of glucose by cells in the liver, well, she just think I'm mad to talk about that. Not be too meaningful in Kitty Queen-Cake land. Topology and Poincare only do be a irrelevancy in a real world person mind. Just be a utterly useless thing to know about. Real world person be that harsh.

And any rate, she not going to be concerned about me. She be too deeply involved in a glossy magazine. Were it the bold letter wording stand out on the cover caught my eye;

SMART GIRLS CARRY COSMO

Were it no real matter, anyone do know that. Were it just a light-read. That were no a criminal issue.

Then the waitress do bring me my cafetiere, and a cup, do it have a little fish painted on the side, and I do be pleased with that. But I be in delay still, coffee have to reach maximum tastefulness just do take awhile. Meantime I try keep away from that Miss kitty Queen-Cake. She might want to scald me with a hot cappuccino.

Anyway were she appearing quite content though, with her looking through her magazine as so, when sonorous bleep sound belong to a mobile telephone then do disturb her intensely concentration. And I just bet she do have a answer machine as well. All real world persons do have one of them. And I just play a chance she do have a lot of technology like that at home. With her skip to the radio were she not have a think about a electromagnetic wave and a Heinrich Hertz, I do know for sure. Why, that Miss Kitty Queen-cake, she not even know Ohm's Law. Were she just having a lot of gall, and listen to the radio like that.

Though I could be wrong, I do know, and be a incorrect idea to have. Were I a real monster to think that way of her. But Miss Kitty Queen-Cake, she, she just make me be so wrathful angry though. Have badly affects on my perceptual acuity. World ought want to lock me in a rogues gallery, with a Jack the Ripper and a Mr Hyde. Be best that way. And I just be a very nasty boy to know.

And I do be ashamed for all that, and it were only a short call anyway. Except that when she did look at me, there were no warning given. No sign for me to look away. Were her gaze just stare right through my eyes at me, and be light with surprisely recognition. And I were all at sea.

'Thought it was you!' Say she, and sit down without asking. Well, Miss Kitty Queen-Cake, she do have a nerve. And the waitress, she do bring her a raspberry patisserie, with a dairy cream on and cow fat. And I do taste sweet sugar in my mouth. And I not like that taste very much.

'Stayed on at school, didn't you?' Say she, at me. 'I didn't. Could have though, 'cause I do be good at that quiz on the t.v., "A Bright Mind", and I be quite good at that.'

Well, she do have a *Encyclopaedia Britannica* at

home and think guide dogs be a good enough way to help blind people. She do have a good sticker on her cardigan which say all that. But she not going to leave me alone though. Were she be showing me a common courtesy with her quite friendly introduction, and explain to me a world which I be outcast, and how her life were going very well with house insurance. And I not want to tell her nothing, how I just be lonely and runaway from my Castalia in the sky. And too be a let down.

'Seen one of these yet?' When she pull out her personal organizer, believe she show a Stone-Age man the wheel. 'They're quite new. It's like a computerized diary.'

All the same, it were the most unnecessary thing I ever see. Were it not for everybody though. Were it only for important people. For those with appointments, and a pressing engagement. Do a unwarranted gadget make a undistinguished person feel important that way. And Liebniz, Boole, a whole lot of information theory, and Shannon and Weaver, did ever foresee anything incomparably splendid. And Miss Kitty Queen-Cake, she say she do own this, she do buy it in a shop. With her calculator mode, and her counterfoils, and her account statement, she were happy doing complex arithmetical operations and a long sums like that. And Blaise Pascal he not own one of these, he be too poor and make his own calculating machine, he be too busy with Pierre de Fermat and throw away his money on a long chance.

It is a very modern world these days, and were they to expire, Miss Kitty Queen-Cake, she just do replace the batteries.

Have her paintly fingernails when she tap on those keys and find out her daytime commitments. 'Look!' Outcry she, 'I must pay my poll tax today.' And when she show me the visual display, were it very first on that list, 'Things to do Today'. And poor grandpop, he be sick with terror and spend interminable hours in Hurricanes and a Spitfire so people not even see tyranny when postman leaves it on the doormat. Not care about it really, just do write a cheque and pay for it. But people be like that though, and not have a worry, and still be unmoved when Black Death and a rat plague do curse Mrs Smith next door. Still only say, 'Thank your lucky stars it's not you Kitty Queen-Cake, Count your blessings it's not you.' And be good enough that way. Because Jesus, He don't love the little children of the world. Let sinners to bleed the poor, and abuse.

Anyway, were I already having a mouthful with her like that, and be in need of a taste of coffee. And were me only about to have a just one sip when, Snakes Alive!, and I do see her shopping basket.

FLY KILLER
KINDLY TO HANDS DETERGENT
ANTI BACTERIAL CLEANSER
DISINFECTANT
BABY LUNG AIRFRESHNER
COMFISOFTLY FABRIC CONDITIONER
VERY STRINGENT BLEACH

Were she having all that kind of stuff there. And

she were going to clean her house with that! And I not know really, were it just no use. Try save a world have a biological war when people not want to save a marine creature from a biological washing powder. Were a Miss Kitty Queen-Cake always be bloodthirsty that way.

So when I look her in the eye, and look for forgiving, were they only like buttons. And not ask a self-question. Just be nothing in a paper eyes. With her unhandsome hoof she only do seize me by the arm and say, 'Help me! must I see that doctor right away. Dermatitis do tingle like mad, and asthmatic respiratory illness going to put me in a early grave.' And the doctor, he just going to shake his head. Write a prescription, then send her away.

But when it do come down to the crunch, and were she do try draw me so close to her. Though she do plea with me. Have she her emptiness eyes, and gently touch my hand. And I do know she going to try slice my wrist with a very sharp knife she just happen to have keep secret from me. I do know she going try kill me.

When hungry blade do swish like lightning, I be too fast for that. Hummingbird sprightliness, with a nature instinct, move me out of the way. And me, I best be out of here, before it be too late for me to leave.

Outside cafe-bar door were I very stranded out in the open. Try cross the square in a serpentine way, try not to flounder, seem be too many animal snares there for me to avoid. Then, unafraid of fast moving traffic, do I runaway straight cross the main road. And flee, fast as I can to the terrace. And don't look back.

Then were I so safe! With my backbone lean close

41

on my blue door. Wait and catch my breath back a bit, and me do feel a little bit remorseful. Were I not wanting to dislike humanly creatures like that. And being so cruel. Were it that Miss kitty Queen-Cake hate human beings that way. Miss Kitty Queen-Cake, she do hate all life.

And me, were I only a disenchanted boy, black sheep and lost his way. Though I do be more worse than that. Be no mistake. I do be more wicked than her, just you wait and see.

THREE

ME do hang on tight in the kitchen doorway, when me were fast deterioration. With worsening condition and all go to the dogs. Because it were a very long way down that hall, and me did rebound a bit on the wall. And were I about to lose a life and whirlpool. Were I not want have the debacle like me have earlier, misadventure and decisive moments. That was truly pioneering. So were I not wishing that to happen.

Pay me deeply consequences, and I've been through the mill, and were my every action now do have to be accurately plan and a well thought out. Oh, if only me were to have some food, and be healthy, and were it a entirely sensible thing to do. But me were having rapidly Valium decay, and it were leading to grave seriousness. Because I not have no more of those. And I not know what to do about that.

And were me very thirsty too. With me never be allowed to have one drink of coffee just now. And me were quite unable to have some food and a water at a one time no more. Were my little stomach be too small for that. And I were everso, everso, starving.

Then me have inclination and go to the pantry. Where me do see a bottle or two of that special beer which I know do belong to poor grandpop. Be the last ones left. And poor grandpop, he know I have to be stealing those. He know I do have to take all those. Be the only thing going to tame me down. Fetch me a glass from the crockery cupboard, and my little bottle-opener, were I like a dog, and sit down in my own chair at the kitchen table. So were nutritive fulfilment going to please the 'hunger-thirst complex' and have me a revamped psychological well-being in a one fell swoop too.

Were poor grandpop's *'Life'* lay unfolded and display all Royal Ascot colours. With ink in selections and racecard he were going to bet all the money he has ever had in his life on the Queen's horse today. And I told him not to do that. But were I only looking through the form when I do become thought provoking and have me resourceful ideas and think I give that manuscript that one last look again. Were I only pushing aside that racing paper and reach out for my article when I do find a little white address card. In front of me, before me, on the table, did it appear. Just happen to be there. And were it simply hiding underneath my sporting newspaper. I picked up the card, and read the invitation;

TO A DR JAMES GRAY

A MR CHALMINGSTON WALMSLEY, DO THIS EVENING AT PARK MANSION REQUEST PLEASURE OF YOUR AUDIENCE. FOR YOU AT SIX A CHAUFFEUR WILL CALL, AND MAKE CONTENT YOUR TRAVEL.

C.W.

And were the little white address card be a real surprise to me. Because Park Mansion were a forgotten castle, lost in a faraway land. Which were very, very, distant from the terrace, and be a long way beyond the square too. Where verdant woodland acres do reach vastly miles and go on forever. A hundred years ago, green and unreal forest did protect wild and untrue beasts from a hungry arrows of knave and king. And in those long ago times, wolves did do wolvely things, and high o'er the river, in blue skies stria yellow-white cloud, larks did ascend.

Even so, were Chalmingston Walmsley having a instructive education and be patron to a fine arts society, and a good friend to the starving children school too. This little, were me glean in a society column in a local newspaper page. So I know he do read philosophical literature and know a few Professors as well.

Only, my life were being very strange recently, and were a person like me do receive bidding to an entertainment at Park Mansion I do think unearthly and macabre. And what were a upper crust want with me anyway. When I were just lowly and a fall from grace, and be quite poor now.

So were I looking at that clock on the wall. Gosh, were it already ten-to-six. And were I quite like to know about this really, and find out what Chalmingston Walmsley want to see me for anyway. Were I finish down my drink too fast though, which make me feel a shred boozy woozy. Then me do run all the way to the front door.

Where me see a motor vehicle was parked in waiting. But it were only a chauffeur driven internal-combustion engine, and I were a little disappointed with that. And were I expecting a coach and horses. So were I a little saddened, and make doubly, doubly, sure the door do lock close behind me, and skip down the garden path. Then climb into the back, and the car do move out of my road.

Were I quite restful in rich upholstery, and were remain inattentive to the world outside and unaware. Until the crimson sun had started its set, and a light mist did lay on the forest floor, and were all the pine trees did be taller than the sky. Then, I did feel quite lost and mislaid. Pressed against the window, and me do try and peer afore. Were there just a mediaevel chateau and a watch-tower made out of stone out there for me to see.

Soonly were the road vehicle pull up on the courtyard of that lithic structure, and the taciturn chauffeur, he do kindly open the car door for me. Where I step out beneath impossible architecture, and look out for the bats. In case there might be a eagle claw swoop down try and take me away. Lucky for me were there a manservant be await on the porch, and he do bid me follow.

Through lobby and hallway he lead me, where there were all mahogany panelling and be newly adorned which did sorrow me. And were the Great Hall too be overly strewn in opulent carpentry and fine joinery, and with the heavily made up drawing-room as well, were just everywhere be so done in *Swietenia mahogoni*. And I did think this very bad, because there were be no trees left in South America.

Meanwhile were I in a magnificent library, towering walls with scholarly writings be all around me. And against the tiers at the far end of the room were there this learned gentleman stand all alone. And he was older than me, in his thirties, and for this evening had chosen dress formal lounge. Plus, when he do notice me, he just do reshelve his literary volume and considerately greet his guest.

'James! You old dog, You!' Do he chant, and shake my hand too. 'Still pushing back the frontiers? Good Stuff!' Were he put on a good show when he do say hello to me, settle me in a luxury easychair, and pour two drinks from a crystal decanter, and he do take good care of me.

'Good Stuff!' say me in pay back glee with a have a first sip of splendid malt whisky which come all the way from Scotland. And watch him be at home in his own easychair.

'Were the whisking brush of Oscar Claude Monet be amour I must proclaim,' he start to say, and treat me to informed exposition on fine art, which were a rare delight for me. 'And when at the gallery this afternoon, were my eyes beheld the most beautiful paintings on canvas, that colours belong to the natural world appear be drab to me by comparison. The Monsieur's work do be that vivid. Those splodges and blobs really be that drastic, phantasmagoric almost, do they actually seem to capture entire vanishing moments. Obviously a radical man with revolutionary ideas.'

So were he only try reassure me how I were in a good company, with him having affinity for fine art, and try and comfort me that way. And were I know how he were having a developed mind and be a warm sentient humanity as well. For sure were I know that, and me do try to talk to him as well.

'Well I quite like *Le Boulevard des Capucines*,' me do happen to say, 'and I quite like that view which he did paint from the studio of Felix Nadar in 1873. Were he just give right to the embracing impression in the *Boulevard*, and Monet, he just do virtually dispense with versed perspective altogether, and objects near and far are seen in accord without spatial separation. Apart from the diagonal line of trees, do perspective in the *Boulevard* just be wholly reduced to colour relationships. And I quite like that. Because Monet, he not only be using colour to create mood with a blue-violet mist and atmosphere, but sensitively too, to portray a sense of distance as well.'

An impressive collection of literature did surround us, when Walmsley cheerily say, 'were I be unfamiliar and not knowing that one James,' and were there just seven eponymous volumes dressed in behemoth symbols, M, O, N, E, T, display themselves upon them bookstacks. And were I feel heartsick and despairing for all that.

Because he were just going to a museum for a cake and some tea, and me do think he were only send out a few birthday cards recently. So were I not have nothing to say. Were I be wondering what this is all about.

Were Chalmingston not show no emotion, just do go right on; with artless lyric he do soon make clear. 'James, both we two have acute affection for fine art and too be sensitive. Much we have in common, you and me. And kindly men as Lord Liverpool be so oft misunderstood. The world is a very cold place to be, and I do mean to change things. Bring back a Six Acts and make all the bad people behave themselves; the world do need sensitive men. That is why, James, I have invited you here this very evening.

'You see, I need you James. I need you to help me make this world a better place to live in. Because were I be a candidate for a municipal Mayor in this district, and were all the people in this town know you be a good grandson to poor grandpop, and were you be a good pupil at the starving children school too and be a reputable scientist now. Were the townspeople, they do know you very well. To the value of your persuasion in a forthcoming election, well, they all be sure to pay a deference.'

And I not feel very chuffed when he do exalt my achievement and overly praise me that way. Because I were not like that. And he do overstate my usefulness in his very strange campaign. When a Dr James Gray not be that notable. Just be a outcast from his castle in the air, and be a total disgrace.

'Mull it over,' came his understand, were he just unable to make of my expression, 'so a commitment do always require of consideration, and were you pledge support to my candidature going to be a real success!' And me, were I not very sure about this, and he just not see this; 'But James, were I not be ungrateful, and to the decision making process I may be of some assist. Because only this morning, Beaky's on the phone, with telling me something good is cooking and a how important friends are. "That Chernobyl matter," he asks, "when were it?" Well, I didn't know and so I was convinced. Were he was only saying how everyone had forgotten, and how an upturn in the nuclear fuels market is soonly occurring. Shrewd purchasing would earn me a bob or two. So my friend Beaky, decent sort, very kindly offered to do the shopping.

'My dear James, were you not need to be too worried, when everything is all perfectly safe. Be no way your money going be chasing a Heath Robinson reactor. Good Grief, no. But believe me James, your concern I quite understand; you go to bed one night, to the retelling of Chernobyl next morning you waken, and shares can't buy a dog biscuit, Can you imagine? Frightening isn't it.

'As far as I can see, Technology, the study and use of the mechanical arts and applied sciences, really is a truly glorious thing James. Technology tried and trusted, truly has made today's nuclear fuels industry wholly failsafe. Were it be a good investment in the future, for everybody's children, everywhere. Made in Britain, were it just sure have to be foolproof.'

Except, with Chalmingston, were there no a trace of underhand sly in his eye, were he not look all sick and devious when he say all this to me. To him be everyday, only average confer and negotiation.

'Very soon will you dispel your apprehension, I know,' were he so assuredly say, 'Man, you are a scientist, after all.' Were then do his plain expression do start to change. And on his face a look did then appear. A look in which his features did show him be attentive and enquiring. 'Then tell me this,' do he challenge, 'tell me this. Just how do a chain reaction work anyway?'

Except, were I not be Enrico Fermi, and all the same, it were a good question. And I quite like to answer him, and do the best I can. So sprightly bound me to the blackboard, happen to be there, where I do choose a fine piece of chalk and try and explain.

'To make clear a scratch understanding of nuclear chain reaction we need accounts of, *The Law of Conservation of Mass-Energy*, *Transmutation*, and *Nuclear Fission*.

'First off, *The Law of Conservation of Mass-Energy*. Albert Einstein recognized that both The Law of Conservation of Mass and The Law of Conservation of Energy were only different aspects of a deeper more general law and set out to redefine mass in the following way.

'The mass of a particle, *m*, is not actually a constant, but always changes with a particle's velocity, *v*, where *v* is the particle's velocity relative to the observer. How the mass of a particle is related to this velocity, and to the velocity of light, *c*, is given by the equation;

$$m = \frac{m_O}{\sqrt{1 - (v/c)^2}}$$

'When the particle m has no velocity relative to the observer and *v* is zero, the ratio v/c is also zero and so the whole denominator reduces to *1*. The equation above then becomes;

$$m = m_O$$

'And so the symbol, m_O, stands for the mass of a particle at rest, or rest mass. Only when the particle's velocity starts towards the speed of light, *c*, does the v/c

term measurably affect the denominator and so affect the mass. As v approaches c, the ratio v/c moves closer to *1*, and so *(1 − v/c)* gets closer and closer to *0*. Thus, the whole denominator approaches to *0*. Were the whole denominator actually to go to zero, then $m = (m_O \div 0)$ goes to infinity. The mass of a particle moving at the velocity of light would be infinitely large, which is a physical impossibility, so the speed of light is a absolute upper limit on the speed any particle can have.

'In a universe where mass changes with velocity, a different understanding of energy was needed if The Law of Conservation of Energy were still to hold. And Albert Einstein supposed that mass and energy are interconvertible; in much the same way as potential energy and kinetic energy. So what is conserved for the energy of a system is all of its forms, including the mass of a system calculated as an equivalent amount of energy; and vice versa. What is conserved about the mass of a system is all of its forms, including the system's energy expressed as an equivalent amount of mass. Hence, The Law of Conservation of Mass–Energy states; The sum of all the energy in the universe and of all the mass (expressed as an equivalent in energy) is a constant.

'When mass converts to energy, the change in energy, ΔE, is related to the change in rest mass, Δm_O, as given in the Einstein equation;

$$\Delta E = \Delta m_O c^2$$

'The velocity of light is extremely large, and its

square far more so, which means even a trace difference in rest mass, Δm_O, corresponds to a extremely colossal value in the change in energy, ΔE. As soon we shall see, with the first observations of nuclear fission the very truth of this equation became quite clear.

'We first need a summary description of *Transmutation*, the conversion of one isotope into another. Observations of this kind of nuclear reaction were first made in 1918 by Ernest Rutherford in the transmutation of nitrogen into oxygen. When nitrogen in an ion chamber was subjected to the action of swift alpha particles (the nuclei of helium atoms) derived from a radium salt, an entirely new radiation was generated. A radiation far more penetrating than alpha radiation, and which proved to be a stream of protons. This reaction is given in the following nuclear equation;

$$\,_2^4\text{He} + \,_7^{14}\text{N} \rightarrow \,_9^{18}\text{F}^* \rightarrow \,_8^{17}\text{O} + \,_1^1 p$$

'So in the transmutation of nitrogen-14 into oxygen-17, the target nucleus nitrogen-14 captures a bombarding alpha particle and a compound nucleus fluorine-18 is formed. This product compound nucleus of fluorine-18 is thus an atomic nucleus carrying excess mass and energy, and is rendered unstable. To be rid of over-sufficient energy, the compound nucleus fluorine-18 has to expel a proton. It then becomes the product nucleus oxygen-17, a rare but stable isotope. In sum, Rutherford was to show his stream of protons came from the decay of compound nuclei of fluorine-18 formed when target nitrogen-14 nuclei captured bombarding alpha particles.

'For sure it was noticed in those early experiments how radioactive changes were very often accompanied by vasts amounts of energy in the form of heat. And very soon it was realized how if arrangements to isolate radioactive materials could be made, and their activities controlled, a new and most important source of energy would be made available to human beings. "The atom has been split," hailed the newspapers of the day, "Energy has been released from atomic nuclei." It was suggested that the Queen Mary could sail many times across the Atlantic on only one ounce of nitrogen, could the energy of its atomic nuclei be utilized.

'When in 1932 James Chadwick made the discovery that neutrons could be knocked out of atomic nuclei, Enrico Fermi in Italy started directing thermal neutrons at a uranium target and studying the radioactive substances formed. By 1939 Otto Hahn and Fritz Strassman finally verified several isotopes much lighter than uranium-235 are formed following this procedure. Barium and krypton for example. Lise Meitner and Otto Frisch were then able to propose Nuclear Fission.

'In *Nuclear Fission*, a nucleus of the isotope uranium-235 captures a slow neutron and a compound nucleus uranium-236 is formed. The product compound nucleus uranium-236 is what undergoes fission and breaks into two roughly equal parts. These two emerging isotopes, say barium and krypton, promptly emit secondary neutrons and so have a total mass slightly less than 236. Now whenever mass disappears, energy is created, as is given in the Einstein equation;

$$\Delta E = \Delta m_O c^2$$

'And as was earlier shown, the velocity of light, $c = 3 \times 10^8 \, m \, s^{-1}$, is a very, very, large sum, and its square, 9×10^{16}, extremely more so. Which means a most trace difference in rest mass, Δm_O, corresponds to a truly monstrous quantity of energy radiated in nuclear fission. Under suitable conditions, when uranium-235 is at or above a critical mass, scientists were soon able to make the process of nuclear fission into a chain reaction. In collisions with surrounding materials the emission of secondary neutrons released in the first fission do again become slow-moving. They too may be captured by unchanged uranium-235 nuclei, which then also do speedily undergo fission, and so it does go. New fissions get to become a very rapid self-sustaining sequence. The energy liberated then produces a terrific explosion, with a temperature of several million degrees immediately after its occurrence. And so, on the second day in December 1942, in a squash court beneath the stands of Stagg Field, a football ground somewhere in Chicago, Enrico Fermi was thus able to activate the first nuclear chain reaction.'

Then with bare face do Chalmingston stand to look at me so soon and say, 'Well, there you have it. A reliable and exacting science make everything very plain and self-evident. British Nuclear Energy is assuredly failsafe.' And were his face be quite undisguised when he say this. To his interest not one word had he found. Though were he who did ask me a question.

And with people were it always that way. Were it always uninformed people who want application of a knowledge for which they have no care. And when that kind of people do hold power and have an opinion, a unmindful recklessness which be both immoral and murderous does always prevail.

So were he not subject to any suffering when he ask of me again, just do make out he doing me a favour and say, 'Put your name down James. You sure can use that helping hand.'

And me, were I want out of here, and feel sick. All the same were I hold on steady to the back of my armchair, because I were really want to burn his house down. Then, were I already on stretched tippy-toes and search all out of the bay windows. And were I feel lucky to see a those headlamps, beam from a front grill of that elegant motor. While me finish up my whisky, plans of a smooth departure do whirl all around in my head. And me then threw him a stare. A stare which have Chalmingston be a prisoner in his own easychair and just say, 'Fuck off and die.'

Were it be best that way.

Though my feet were really a untamed cheetah paw, and they were have me out of there in a microsecond. Far-flung through them passageway corridors me were outside in the night quite fast and fly towards the motor vehicle. Then me hopped very neatly into the back, and let the road machine make a very speedily desertion. And when the car do glide out along that driveway and me do turn and through the rear window stare. Were there this demolished figure stand by himself in the doorway of Park Mansion and being unhappy. With dancing mania he just do wave his arms in a rage. Though it be ineffectual.

But the night-time was fall down around me, and the loneliness I did seek were not so far away now. And so soon were the car arrive at the terrace. Where it did stop outside my blue door. And me, were I jump out. Were the quiet driver, he just do drive away, leave me be alone on the street. Where me were look up at the stars. Because were my life be a real nightmare now.

FOUR

So were me in the kitchen and lonely place, were a 60 watt bulb be a light on me. With the day have be a disaster and the world won't go away. And were I like me be withdrawn like this and isolation, and wish me have a aloneness when I feel this way. But were my little head a quiet rest in my palms, and again were me staring at a solely manuscript, while the night was outside my window.

CELLULAR STUDIES OF NEURONAL FUNCTION IN THE HORSESHOE CRAB *(Limulus)*.

The paper were only a description of a most recent experiments, and it have be ready for submission to *The Journal of Comparative Neurology* for a long time now. And were the horseshoe crab not a real crab, nor even a spider even. Were it just be in a animal kingdom class by itself, *Xiphosura polyphemus*, and just have a horseshoe shaped shell and a long tail-spine as well. And anyway, were these findings only be a small potatoes in the scheme of things in any case. And even so, were studies do enquire upon the structure and function of neurones in a unnoticed marine invertebrates not be trivial.

Any understand of the action of the nerve impulse only be through a careful investigations and a meticulous researches into the ionic basis of resting and action potentials and the control of cell membrane permeability in a squid axon. Which did be a hard work and a worthwhile experiments of Hodgkin, Huxley, and Katz, and their schools. Except, were a frog neuromuscular junction and a vertebrate preparations be a useful things to study as well. Be in a history after Otto Loewi and a Henry Dale, were a elucidation of the nature of chemical transmission across synapses only come from the school of Katz, del Castillo, Fatt, and Miledi. And were the clarification of gamma amino butyric acid be a neurotransmitter in the nervous system of the lobster found out by Kravitz, Hall, Kuffler, Potter and Otsuka, did only ever lead to further discovery of new transmitter substances.

Because to make clear the activity of nerve cells only come from a deep down need which seek a explanation of nature. Be a true real need understand nature, be the causation of detailed researches as these. And to bring creative things into physical existence only come from long shot and calm endurance with what is unshaped and intangible, and which may never, ever, be demonstrable, or be actual. And were this, bring rudimentary idea into physically existing creative things. Were only in consequentiality to pure researches, technologies as medicine do ever exist. It can only be that way. This is why scientific enquiry into the physiology of quiet marine invertebrates and difficult phenomena not be trivial.

But scientific enquiry to most people not be very interesting. Pure researches be too abstract for them to care about. Though a visible application and perceptible technology people do cherish and value, do be to them quite useful. You can sell technology. Be very powerful, and rule the world. And from where do pretty fuck do they think all this does materialize?

Were a person in the real world not want to know.

Except, were a person in the real world have every right to be that way. And were a those rights, those freedoms given to a person by the laws of the world into which they were born. But sometimes were a real world person be too satisfied with their own freedoms. And were they be content with always having material and owning other people like that. And were they not care because they do have those rights that many others do have none. Though even in their own contentment were those freedoms given to a people in the real world not be immutable. Too were those freedoms forever being defended or taken away with fighting and changing law, and so be uncertain that way. And in his own contentment were a real world person not see that either. Do he just do take his entire world for granted.

So in a real world lifestyle, must every person only do as their own conscience bids. Must every person look into their own heart and be as they feel. And because in a real world lifestyle every person does have his own personal rights, and too does look deeply into his own heart, in the end, do plain ignorance always triumph over good reason.

Those unwished occurrences fill up my day have me feel this way. With a those two persons I have met today were it always that way. Were they only reaffirming everything I did already know. So wildly unreasoning, were there no scope for learning. About them were they only have their carelessness, which do only be causing a unforeseen harm. And so; what do be providing useful material to these people in a real world and exercise their freedoms?

The answer were only creative thinking. Were only pure researches sustain all the material in our real world. So were I have to be destroying this manuscript then. Where me do take the unsuspecting paper and rest down on my knees at the fireside grate, appear be a matchbox there await for me do some harm. But me were doubtless some dab hand would soon happen on identical findings, were it happen already be no surprise to me. Would anything useful surface in my mind a long time ago occurred in a imaginative person mind. Be it as so, were me not be the kind of animal to give scientific discovery to those who murder and abuse. Were me not be that bad. And so, me, were I just struck that match. While careful written pages lay useless in the grate. Were I just struck that match and set fire to them all. And I watched those flames burn them unseen papers. In the night I watched them burn and be so heartless. Were those burning embers just vanish into smoke and away to the chimney flue did disappear. And that was it. Gone. Were a untold discovery just be unknown.

Then me did have one last drink left on the table. Dreadful ringing in my ears am I forever in wakeful exhaustion. Sleep too were be removed from my life. With tiredness open very last beer bottle and make me start for bed.

Remains and pieces of me climb up them stairs,

and try not to disturb poor grandpop. Drowse instinctual, were I not worry about undressing, and fall right into bed. With pillows keep up my sleepy head and sipping drink for comfort, when heavy eyelids begin to fall. And then in catnap my head do dive, and jump me back to being wakeful, and I do start to yawn. Extremely soporiferous influence and overwhelm me, were me just have to lay down my sleepily head now. Drown rat, and abandon to narcosis.

Parasympathetic effect make my beating heart rate get very slow, and soon have me in a slow wave sleep. Plus, were my only breathing lungs be quite gradual now as well. And me, were I have no sense of night-time, and seem me were have a loss of consciousness for ever. But then, demeanour in my own physiology happen to change things a bit. Were it quite unannounced, and causing sharp difference in my somnia. With rapidly breathing can be erratic, were a wide sympathetic activation all at once betide me; and my heart do start to race a piece. Though all the time I do be very sleepful.

And then I find me wander in a unknown world. Where me do happen upon a very thin angel with a broken wing, who too be disenchanted, and have sorry in his eye. His eyes did so tell me this, for to me were they just a mirror, and cruelly reflect a unhappiness which be inside of me. And how he too just be an outcast, and fall from grace. Look so heavily worn out and tired, do he so have a story he want tell me. Which do unfold a foolishness we both be fallen prey to. Have he this handwritten volume carry with him, and listen to his disheartening tale I do agree.

THE
PERSONAL
HISTORY
OF
JAMES GRAY

WERE there once existing a boy, who did be very poor stricken and have hungriness. And though he were so very young, and only a starveling, were he very inspirited and have fiery dreams. For were this hungriness, which he did have, merely a actual need to be understanding nature. Were he be so hungry, were to seek and make plain and detail naturally occurring phenomena his sole reason to live.

Whereabouts one day, when he was still a manchild, were he sent quite far away to a castle in the sky. Where he did listen to many professors, and learn and read a great many things, and this in time he came to see: That mankind be best understood in the terms of his history, and that the development of the individual too may be seen within this context.

And about human complexion, to him this did seem quite true. Because, that man best be understood in the perspective of the centuries allows account for human progress through the ages. And were this sustained advancement of humankind through the years owing to a ceaseless acquisition of knowledge. But were this boy who have hungering, and want understanding of the material and functionings of the universe so badly, soon come to recognize this as well: To a large degree, though not entirely, were history showing this sustaining of human furtherance be mainly attributable to scientific endeavour.

And in truth, were a fascination in science capture him and have him feel this way.

So, in this way of thinking, which he came to have, were the personal development of any individual too seen in the perspective of the centuries. Though his supposing were not deny a living soul have his own distinctive character and be his own person in every way. Only, that the growth of a individual person be seen in the historical setting in which they do live. Were himself, for instance, always have a hot drink every sunrise, run water from a tap and switch on a kettle. So were he use material application all the time, and this he did take as given. Except, were this a kind of selfishness, and just being self-centred really. For were he not have to care a flowering knowledge keep him alive. But were a poor person living in long ago times not have these kind of things. So seen in this way, when he forget it were a ever growing knowledge bring providence into his life, were his own living just be very egocentric.

And so, because history were show the scientific endeavour be central to the improvement of human existence, were the hungry boy begin to see, how the development of his own personhood too were dependent on his own abilities as a scientist to interpret this world he was born into.

Were other people too, construe their worlds as scientists, he likewise supposed. And for certain, were every individual person comprehend the world in his own way, as well. Besides, life is characterized by the creative capacity of a individual person to interpret the universe in his own way, and so, different persons simplify the universe in different ways. And since the universe owes no loyalty to any one person's understanding, so were it ever open to re-evaluation. And were the starveling know this. Were the very nature of knowledge be dynamic, and always do it change with new discovery and be mutating that way. As both scientist, and sentient being, he did be aware of this. That all of his understanding about the universe were open to revision and replacement he did be fully aware. Though were this no a problem. Because were a scientist always seek a new explanation, alternative, and other options. And as every personal being do seek an understanding of the world they were born into, so then do the aspirations of all persons be essentially those aspirations of the scientist. Were he have a empathy with other human beings tell him this be so. For were a mankind being just be a incipient scientist.

Chosen with this way of thinking were the hungry boy having some fair understanding of human complexion, and too his own living soul, and into his life were this bring much structure and balance. The regard with deep respect in which he held scientific endeavour were absolute. For were his life have purpose and be meaningful owe to scientific studies and pure researches. With strong sense of direction and have good intention, were he spend all the time in his castle in the sky and do experimental investigations. So to scientific endeavour were he just give his solely devotion.

Only, were there a day come by were he make a discovery which be to him very harrowing. Were a unveiling about human complexion and were a self-discovery as well which he not like very much. And one he had not seen for his own feeling comfortable and living unconsidered. Because if human scientific endeavour be deem truly entitled to so veneration, then were he too as effective scientist, and merely human being, truly being seen in the same estimation. So were so an admiration for mankind accomplishments only be a vanity.

And when choosing to understand mankind ways in the perspective of the centuries, the truth of his own immodest thinking were he starting to feel. Only were knowledge not be the only measure of mankind history. And were this a wrongful impression to have, and just be too assuming. With desperate cruelties were history books always being completely filled. About responsible and progressive intellectual beings were they be very harmful.

Then were this lost hungry boy just be a victim of his own opinionated reasoning. And so to see humankind in the terms of history as wholly reasoned and creative lifeforms were only ever his own preconceived opinion and just be a conceit. And were he miss to see all this, come from his own feeling content and being a ivory tower person. So whenever were he look into his own heart, were he see how his own hypocrisy and his own vain intellect come from his

66

own satisfactoriness. And were a ivory tower person the same as a real world person.

And when were he see how all his firm belief in humanness were only a arrogance, and just be sophism and a Devil's trick, were he have to leave his only castle in the sky and be a outcast. Disenchanted, were the world all fall away. With the lonely story come to a close, were he just be a living soul without belief. Awaiting James Gray were there only nothing. Despair in utter hopelessness were all there ever was.

All the same, were me return into my own lost and irreparable world, and in my bedroom were I wake up from a drowsy sleep. But sadly fatigued were me lay very lame in some emotional trauma and feel very thirsty as well. Were I turn over though, and glimpse of the clock, and 5.40 p.m. do astound me. And my heart do jump pace, and crave affection. Were I be asleep all that time! So were the daytime nearly gone and I better get out of bed.

So thirsty were me sway to the wardrobe, where I do stare at my very dry tongue in the mirror, and were it just be a good thing to do. Devise of a simple plan somehow take place in my mind, but were I always think very carefully about what me will be doing next. With my dipsomania inflamed, were me evaporate in a hot shower seem be advisable. Lead me into severely dehydration and make me want to have just one drink. And were the Summer evening sun fall incident on my mirror and show how my star-crossed destiny were just to walk by the river and find some booze. Somehow were I always be a wayward.

FIVE

DANCE beneath a fading solar sky were me down on the waterfront, and watch the two swans swim out to a river island, where eels do live as well. Even so were my eyes see sundown reflections and chromatic aberrancy, so I knew there was magic in the air when I was way back in the town square. But then were me near the end of the promenade, where the roadway do turn and leave the river behind.

So were me follow that roadway, and pass by the Royal Park, where kind fallow deer do stand grazing on the flora, which be all they ever do have for a evening meal. And were the leafy byway meander gently, and lead me very far away. Where very many trees and verdure bring me close to a woodcutter's cottage, and remind me to keep a look out for a hungry wolves. Then the embrace of twilight were fall all around me, and I do lose my way a little.

Though me were see a radiance soon, which like a candle glow, and want to take a closer look. Were it just a soft flicker in the distance, and be warm like a lantern in a forest under a spell. So were I in a hurry to find out for myself, and in no time were me outside peer through a window at the lamplight tavern.

Doorway hang faded blackout curtains when I walk in, and deep inside, me were know I want a drink. And the landlord were very kind to me,

'Evening,' all he say to me, and pour for me a pint. Except were this a extra special beer and, 'On the house,' he sure insist. But were me very pleased with that and say thankyou. Only, me were very drink thirsty and were want another one soon. Because it were taste sweet and honey and make me feel happy again. Still, the landlord, he do kindly refill my glass, and again he not want no money off me. And were this unusual to me, though I were quite content to go and sit somewhere quietly alone.

And deep inside, were me know I have to have that drink and were being unable to give it up without incurring adverse effects very badly.

But scattered assemblies somehow have me in a surround, and were me hear voice sound confusion without actual words all the time. And were there these two people prop up the bar, with overly loud conversation and very high volume. Be a impressive briefcase full of paper have the young man wear a suit, while the elderly, more distinguished gentleman, he were forever puff on a cigarette.

'Working?' Ask the young man in a suit.

'Work?!?' Say the old man surprised. 'Are you mad?!? Course I don't work. Why should I work when I can stay in the pub all day? You think I'm stupid?'

And were he annoyed by this, and fly his cigarette zigzag in the bar room sky. And frown, and be displeased. Were his name called Apples, Charlie Apples, because me were listen to the landlord address him as so, and balance undecided he was wavering a bit. As he wavered, were ash always fall from his cigarette. Though it were only ever burn holes in his own apricot crimplene trousers, with a blue blazer, and ruin his own carpet space as well. 'Course I don't work,' he were say, 'Got more sense. Peasants and morons work.'

So were he in a rocking-horse poise, and try scrutinize focus on the far away clock. While may-care whisky remains await on the counter.

'Ants ll be in soon,' he do say to his friend. 'Bleeding Friday Night morons. Work all the time, running round like tiny bleeding ants, don't see em in ere all week. Catch the tube, go home, "How are you dear?", then what?...Friday Night. Must go down the pub. "Ere Harry, Friday innit? Must go down the pub and talk shop." Cor, can you imagine? Only been at work all week. They're just like ants! Tiny bleeding ants!

'Friday Night. Don't ever see em in the week. True! Only come out in injury time, when he rings on the bell. They're all Mad! I mean, why bother? I mean, why go down the pub when it's time to go home? Don't make sense do it? They're all raving mad!

'Thing is, the peasants can't afford to do it, haven't got it. "Yeah, coming down the pub?" "Oh, why's that then?" Haven't got it. Only been at work all week. Haven't got it. Gotta get out that Mickey Mouse Barclay Card. See a bloke in ere once, poor devil had to write a bleeding cheque pay for a drink. Never seen anything so ridiculous in all my life!'

All the time have he one eye pin down the young man in a suit, when he sip whisky and say all this. Who seemed to be lacking vigour, and not like a good conversation. Though Apples not care about that.

Were he have gazely pupil and stare out his friend look unsettle, and gruffly say, 'Go home with your Barclay Card! Go home and play ludo with the wife! Minnie ll be waiting to pay the mortgage and cook a business lunch. Go on, go home!'

So were the young man wear a suit not have to listen all this. Perhaps he really do have some other place to go; What do I know? So he just left quite quietly. Leave Apples stand all alone at the counter, fag ash fall down everywhere.

To the bar mirror were he then turn, do a king lion then stare back. Were he have his silver grey hair, cut short and comb back, and with a little grease, and look very neat. And were he be most clean shaven as well, and like me, were I imagine he just always be that way when in the pub. Like his apricot crimplene trousers, with a blue blazer, were his yellow silk tie wear with a dirty filthy polka dot shirt too be wore in mismatch. For in truth he were immaculately groomed, and very good at dressing as well, that it did so notice. On the counter, by his glass collection, were a unclean plastic bag. And me did wonder what use a gentleman of his verve were have for a thing like that. For although so irregular, and so far-away, were Apples actually be, all the time were there existing around him very real likenesses. Likenesses in a unseen being which did be to me most unaccountable, and make me feel quite restless. So were I have to think carefully about him.

'Lemsip!' To the landlord he implored. With additional whisky tumbler were he be plied. Though he were soonly sway, with his awkward halting gait, and go out into middle of the bar room floor. Where all the pub hearsay say how the hip wound were a keepsake of his from when serving His Majesty over in North Africa in 41. But then some other overhear just say it was a bad misfortune he not see that motor car when leaving the pub one night. So with him limp out into lonely bar room space, were he have nightingale beguile and start to sing.

Truly beautiful music were sound from a syrinx in his throat, while he do manage a lemsip and one fag in just one hand, and let his supermarket bag swing softly in the other. So were a graceful birdsong I be listen to, when more beer to the table do the landlord bring. Which really do be humanitarian.

Alas were the nightingale song eventually stop. And at my table, the old desert rat do falter and fall down in a chair.

'Happy days,' were me say quite thankfully, because somehow me were know all this plentiful beer do be a wild philanthropy of his.

'Pleasure, young Gray,' were he say back, and incidentally use my name like that, 'not oft you see a gentleman in ere. Just idiots mainly. Only the other day this fella walks up to me and says; "Hello Charlie! I like you, you're a real character. Pubs have got a have a character, and I like characters." See Gray, bleeding idiot. Pub characters? Ain't no such things. Just misfits, that's all. Bleeding misfits.'

And that he knew me well quite startle me actually, and make me feel worry and concern, because were the brain be quite forgetful these days. So sip beer and listen were all I ever decide to do.

'Tell yer young Gray, had a drink in ere eleven

o'clock this morning with an old fella, name of poor grandpop. Not a bleeding soul in ere! Bloody ridiculous it were, only people in ere. So I says to poor grandpop, "Cor Blimey! Where have all the people gone? They can't all be having a party." You see, I don't understand it. The pub's open all day, and no one wants to have a drink. It don't make sense.

'And yet when it gets late and the good landlord decides to lock up and go to bed, what happens? All them bleeding ants walk in, thousands of em, and expect to buy a drink. Why is that then Gray? I don't understand it. Pub's open all day. Why is that?'

Were Apples then take a drink from his lemsip, while a old-time cigarette lay quietly die in a ash tray. Were he then unwrap a Fox's glacier mint as well and appear be philosophical. And me, were I just wonder how he do know my only poor grandpop. Since the existence of so a being, he surely would mention.

'You do see it in ere all the time though. Only the other evening this fella's standing at the bar; "Gimme six pints of bitter will yer, and a large brandy for Rose. And Daisy wanted a gin, Maud wanted a snowball, ...er, with a cherry in, and Juliet, Juliet? What did Juliet want? Ol yeah, whisky cola for Juliet, and one for yourself and the lady wife."...Good bloke, yer see.

'Anyways, next morning, see the same bloke standing at the bus-stop. Well, I go up to him; "Scuse me sir, you got 8op for a loaf of bread?" "Please sir," I said, "You got 8op, I'm hungry." "8op!" he goes, "8op! Are you mad!" Yeah Gray, same bloke who was in ere treating everybody, "Are you mad!" he said, "You think I got money to throw away." And then his little boy walks up; "Dad! Dad! Can I have a couple of bob go to the Strawberry Fair?" "What you wanna go to the Strawberry Fair for, you think I'm made of money?" And there he was! Waiting for a bus! Cor! Can't catch a cab, can he. Ain't got the money. "What you wanna waste your money go to Strawberry Fair for?"'

And Apples, who be so old, with paper and tobacco were he just roll another cigarette; 'Tiny ants, Gray. All of em. Tiny ants.'

Then for a moment were he hesitate, and be very thoughtful. Were a fresh cigarette on his bottom lip naturally adhere. 'Then, tell me this,' he do say all of a sudden, and take me by surprise, 'Why do all the physical properties and complex interactions of matter and energy peculiar to the far away galaxies and all the universe sustain our existence?'

No way a answer I do have.

'Tell you why,' were he say, very serious and grave. And just use twenty pounds to light his cigarette, and sternly say; 'When you got money, Gray, when you got money, you are the nicest bloke in this pub. When you got money, you do as you please. You only ever see a moron wait for a bus and be salt of the earth.'

And that were make the world go round.

Were those steely eyes and bitter just stare at me, yellow-ochre fingers clutch a plastic bag, have all the money in the world. 'You see Gray, whenever you meet someone, could be a blindman, or a valentine, it don't matter. Always this you must be thinking; "How can I get your money into my pocket?" This you must be thinking, all the time.

'Because, young Gray, wheresoever you may roam, them tiny bleeding ants will be thinking exactly same thing. Take the other morning, down the market, "Luverly juicy oranges, five for a quid." All them greedy buggers think, "Bargain." Well, what do I want five bleeding oranges for. I only want one. It ain't like I got scurvy. So I gives the boy on the barrow 20p; "Can't do that," he says, "30p". See Gray, never give anything away for nothing.'

Disdainful were he inhale hard on his cigarette, and believe in every word he say was true, then rub out dog end in the ashtray dirt. 'Anyone can make money,' he do tell me, 'anyone. Don't ever need to have had one idea in your head, just be good at bleeding people.' And were those yellow-ochre fingers then reach into that precious supermarket bag; 'Give you a clue,' were he say, and affix to his skull do he a most ridiculous article I ever did see.

A real live headband it were! With two very long wibbly-wobbly antennae, and were both aerial feelers have a star shape at the end, and just do leap bounce everywhere. A head like a moth were Apples just have.

'Stupid, innit,' were Apples say quite plainly. 'Well, this ere object can be no possible use to man nor beast. Yet when a couple of idiots start wearing these down the Wag Club, then the whole blimmin world got to have a pair.'

So were that a scam of his. And it did be a good surprise to me. For were I remember a long time ago, in the nineteen-eighties, were everyone just wear insect aerials like these for all Summer and be mooncalf. Were it just so fun for everyone to do.

And were Apples be the wicked man who invented all the rubbish in the world, I did think be a wrongful thing to do. Because were he re-invent the diary and call it a filofax and rob not very bright people that way. Were people like useless hamburger sandwich though, Ronald MacDonald do know that. So were Apples remove that foolish article from his weary head and be incredulous of any human goodness.

'Who cares?' Were he ask me. 'Nobody. Fucking nobody cares about nothing. So don't make the mistake that they do. Remember that, Gray. Care only for yourself. Because nobody else goin to.'

So rise to his feet, were he stand oblique to the vertical, no more do he say to me. Were he have all a glaze eyes, and the bar-room door were hard to find. And were he just leave. Drag away his money in a plastic bag and inside, were Apples just laugh at the day.

Then were I watch him disappear through faded blackout curtains, quietly drink alone, and me were know I be like that. Because me were have no faith in human sincerity anymore, and too be quite contemptuous of a human living soul. Though were Apples have those awkward likenesses, and somehow be familiar and unaccountable, did be forewarning to me. And were he know my poor grandpop, and be *Picture of Dorian Gray*. Then me were know I meet a *Christmas yet to Come* and have very sick karma.

SIX

THEN me were out in the darkly night, empty and black, try and crawl home drunk. And were a lonely star sparkle in the sky for me. Though the highway not look too good anymore.

Because were the wild forest all gone. Were only thin trees left and have no foliage. Which do worry me a little. With no freshly leafiness and the wild forest all gone were the world only be isolation and dendritic skeletons and uninhabited skies.

Wholly bewildered, me were walk through diffuse arborizations silhouette landscape and disbelieve all this. And were me just stare down into the fracture and brokenness which were draw very heavily in a stone path underfoot. But were all the damp mosses and very hard lichen too be vanish from a shattered flagstone path. So were I want to take a closer look and wander away from the roadside and into the wood. Afraid by scattered dead trees were the wood seem quiet and cold, so were me be careful not to go too far away from the road. And me were only hoping to see just one living thing. Except me were even look under burn to ash leaves and all the dry timber as well. But were the saprophyte fungi and everything, too all gone away! Then me were know the renewal of plain nitrogenous material necessary to a green woodland survival were just not going to happen anymore. So me were run back very fast to the road and the world get scarier.

Only were me start to think if this truly and really be a right way home. For owe to my eyes were stained with inkiness were I not catch sight of much in the dark. So whereabouts am I, me do guardedly feel. And anyway, Death Angels were fly very high o'er me. Way up high, close to a lonely star sparkle where I can't see. Were me just know they be there. And me were awaken pace, and slightly flee. Oh hurry home I must!

Were something do stop me though. Were something lay down in the roadside gutter and make me stop and look. And were my heart feel low. Where me were stare at two pheasants just lay to waste. Listless, and unfolded, and just be rubbished mass. Though in my crazy depression, in colour were I somehow see them; bright scarlet faces, and chestnut plumage all handsome mark in cream and black, with iridescent green sheen and purple which were intensify at the nape. Only, were they just be dead. Soundless, cold, and worthless remain.

Cross to the other side, were me run away again. And step beneath the serious wall enclose the Royal Park. Were the wall very high though, and have unearthly silence seclude everything from the outside world. And too have solemn promise. Tower way above me, Death Angels do start a line. Were a night frost bite sharp on my fingertip. Death Angels were want to do me harm.

So were me want to reach the park entrance, where the cast iron gates do stand tall. Be close to the river there. While woodland beasts and wild creatures in the park were cry a little. And me were want to try and help them. With me run to the gate, hold on to the foundry iron and stare out into stringent lands and darkness. Where me not see anything at all. Then me were use my whole body weight, lean down on those heavily loaded gates, and push me a way through.

Hesitating steps me were make in this park, unseeing and don't know where I'm going. Carefully me were wander out in inhospitable plains, and see the lines of scarified dead trees strew out in the far away. And me were feel danger, and were my lungs just breathe on a raven air. And me do stand quite still for a while and listen. When suddenly wild animal do cry, and me were feel it suffer. And were it cry with fading lameness and wound, and so the sounding never came back.

Have me sharp senses and look everywhere for my wild creature in this unfavourable world, but me were too late. And feel sorrow. Woodland animal just lay maimed on the ground. And me did see the animal were only a young deer fawn then. A young deer fawn shot down and wait for fate. Then me were fall down on my knees with no good aims of doing something to help. Only stay with the deer were all I could do, for were the creature lay helpless there on the ground. And me were watch the deer fawn, see the last breath fade into a condensation in a careless night air. Touch lightly the young fallow deer coat, in a high starry sky and just feel hopelessness. And I were watch that deer fawn die. Watch very last sparkle fade from deer fawn eye.

Then lonely sapphire glints and the pale moon were cast clouds inside a young animal eyes, permanently wide iris and ashen lustre. Were the faintly moon only uncover their absolute lifelessness. Dead creature coat have gone cold, and my bloodstained hand have turned dry. And those fallow deer antlers, short pronged, and not yet branched, were a tell to me of how the young deer just about live and see a second year, so me were feel the taste of iron in my mouth. Because that deathly blue tincture were underneath that dead creature coat, thoroughly washed out and stain all other colour of anatomical complexion inanimate white.

And with my hand touch the dead animal skin, and touch the killing wound, a very slow death all the time were me just think about. And one last look at wasted deer fawn were make a unwanted picture memory in my mind, and just be a fallow deer slain down on cold grounds. And I just walk away and be downhearted.

Though out in the far away, cover in the frightened trees, Death Angels were want me. And when they so wish, it do have to be that way.

Back standing at the iron gates were me feel in sorrow. My feet were somehow drag me there. Were me leave the park behind and not look back, though deer fawn picture memory I know I won't escape. So close to the river me were see waterfront railings reach to the very end of the promenade, and walk a long distance on the quay. The silver moon were shine so gently on quiet water, were the river seem unusual and calm. And this were make a disturbance in me.

Climb onto the rails and down the quayside wall me were stare. And were all the fish lay in dirty water and look ghostly pale. Were me see them sick and dying, and make me more unhappy. Were me just look and have despair.

But were dark motions capture in the side of my eye. Were a Death Angel dance on the rails, long way, park end. Only were me not care anymore. With me look down like that, and the moon on the water, were the river somehow want me. And then deer fawn picture memory do appear. Much like a painting in a candle flame were it just appear and make me feel wretched. And again me were see a young fallow deer slain to no purpose and lay worthlessly in the cold. Then very plain were the picture memory make it, how ignorance and violence just be the same thing.

Because in the picture memory were the deer only lay to waste, and that a woodland animal too be possessed with the quality of having life were the killer not care about. That a heart beat in a wild creature chest were have a physiology comparable to the physiology of his own heart were he not give a careful thought to. Were he pay no attention to that. Just do take away a animal life needlessly.

Then very clearly me were see; Violence were only to act harmfully against something, and to act harmfully against something is to disrespect it. And to disrespect a thing is to have intentional disregard, and so; violence is plainly ignorant.

But were the inverse true as well; Were ignorance only a choosing to remain in unknowing, and were a refusing to take notice only to have intentional disregard. And to have intentional disregard, is not to respect something, and treat as of no importance. And to disrespect a thing is to act harmfully against it, and to act harmfully against a thing were only to violate it. Then consequently, me were see; ignorance is fell violence.

Though even more macabre it really were, for wild creatures really do be living things. Even so, maybe the killer were try and make easy some understanding of a fallow deer existence. Maybe he were say man's place in nature do be, as if by some divine sanction, to have dominion over all other worldly creatures and that is a good way to get along. Or maybe he were have some discernment of a animal kingdom which were place the feral beast to a taxonomic order way beneath the primates in some strange *Scala natura*. All the same, were this just be convenient simplification really. Because the killer were only see a fallow deer liveliness as quite inferior to his own vivacity and treat a wild animal as undeserving of life. And he will be quite judicial about this, and divorce himself from the glaring knowing he is destroying a living creature.

And were this considered derogation make purposeless slaughter uncomplicated.

And with each other were people like this, and be so derogatory. To each other were they remove all sensitivity from their victims and be very degrading that way. And this were help alleviate any conscience of wrong doing. In that violation be of no concern when the victim not be a sentient human being.

Though were people violent like this to their own selves as well. Because sometimes were a person try and separate his own living soul in two, and see himself divided with having two opposing elements. For instance, maybe he were see his own sense of reason diametrical to his own emotionality and account for his actions that way. And were his head sometimes rule his heart. Only were this quite harmful with a person see his own rationality estranged from his emotions like that and hurt his own karma. Since this too were only convenient simplism, and a human living soul were more involved than that. Owe to human intellect were really a mixing of good reason and real feeling too, and countless other energies and infinite imaginations. So that Euclid could feel intensely about triangular space, and human creativity were not really dichotomized as so and cruelly tear apart.

But even clever persons were sometimes have a 'good me' and a 'bad me', and look for understanding in a psychological medicine which be very deceiving sophism, and very harmful to a soul life too, and not let a person look into his own heart.

Then suddenly my picture memory were change slightly, and me were watch the fire dance in a candle glow. And me were see a strange dreamlike variation. For all at once were there a hunter appear, who do only ever kill deer for a meal and who were familiar with the deer and their forest domain. So were he know something about a fallow deer and too their woodland surround. Have he know of a fallow deer diet, and how they do browse on herbage, shrubs and young tree shoots, and too acorns and chestnuts. That fallow fawns mostly be born in May or June, and usually in a close retreat far in among the bracken. Plus in the Winter, and during the breeding season, fallow deer do be very often encountered in herds of both sexes whilst at other times in parties of bucks or does. All these kind of things he were just know about. Since the behaving of his game, and also the woodland habitat in which these creatures do thrive, he were find interesting and make much study about.

So were this hunter be quite sparing with what he does kill, and have a awareness forbidding slaughter get too needless. Were he not kill more than he do need to eat, nor were he eat more venison than he do be prepared to kill. Because even a most dispassionate killer were know what creatures he do slay today were not be there tomorrow. So to the fallow deer, and too the woodland habitat which do uphold a fallow deer survival, he must give some respect.

Then he were see in the wooded countryside, much interaction, and much interdependency, between all the animals and all of the plants as well, and too between all of these lifeforms and the nature elements. Moreover, to living things the hunter were have sensitivity, and Nature he were try and understand.

And when it do come to the killing time, he were feel that terrible heart race, and be very anxious. Because he were have that unmistakable knowing he were destroying a animal life. And he were know that animal will bleed and cry. So were he have to look very deep into his own heart. Were he have to be seeing through all that well meaning argument, and be owning up to himself. Because when that arrow fly, he may go to Hell.

Though real world persons not ever have to mindfully kill animals, just do go shopping. All the time were they feast on meat and be so unforgiving.

And it is people who do this though. People who have their own dreams and not hurt a fly. Were they not want to kill a animal.

So were it always the way, were people not really want to re-examine things and ask a self-question. Were they be happy and know what's right and wrong. Even so, were satisfactoriness and wilful disinterest just be hateful.

But then my picture memory were start to fade, grow lightly faint and quietly disappear. Lateness moon just wash it away. And then some other inexplicable picture telling just do betide in my thinking, and an old man on a railway train me were start to see. He was sitting all alone in an empty compartment when a young couple entered, uncombed, and not too well dressed. Were the old man not seem very pleased when they sit down opposite, and how it is that people without 1st class tickets are not allowed to sit there to the two he does try and explain. Only some accounting too does the young man try and offer, and say how they also pay for a seat but only have money for 2nd class and how the rest of the train do be full up, and were the young woman soon expecting a child as well. All his life have the old man been hearing excuses, and so he not see why he should pay a 1st class fare when they two just be committing an intentional offence. So were the old man only want what is fair and calls out to the ticket inspector. Then do the situation really start to flare. Because the young man he have rage and spit vehemently at the old man, and this two officers happen to see; and they do descend hard on the young man before they make an arrest. And in a strange land where democracy do uphold segregation of 1st and 2nd class peoples on a transport network which every person do have a equal owning in, all this were taking place. Then, with this depiction of police apprehension were this impression too just vanish, and only leave me watch ignorance and violence cumulate into more. Since in so a world without careful thought, nor any real feeling for others, were ignorance and violence just escalate into indecipherable madness.

Whereabouts were this leave me stand alone on the quayside and be so useless. But me were try and care about pollution, and a unworried intellect which have done all this. Though me were have good intentions and be clever thinking too. So were I always lying to myself with a incorrect argument and make for harmful remiss. So were me like to suit myself, and be quite evil really. Death Angels do know that. And I see them on the rails and just wait for me.

SEVEN

WERE the sun very yellow in the azure skies and deeply blue. In a daybreak cold, and were the night pass slow. Tired and out, were me still stranded against the rails with the tide gone out and misty morning. With my life energy removed, carelessly lost in a first light cold.

Were she just standing, at the churchyard wall across the road. And when I saw her, with her neglected appearance and long crimson dress, were she start walking towards me. Her hair was black, and her face looked young, and I thought she was quite pretty. Were she look at me with her dark eyes and I were crave her affection.

Then when she took my hand, with the touch of her warm fingertips were she foresee a star-crossed destiny wait for me. And when I look into her eyes again were they somehow tell me this, and how she too were long for affection and be so alone. With her look at me so desperately and her hand hold tight were she place this small notebook in my open palm, and me were do anything she say. So when she kissed me, then slowly let go of my hand, she were break my heart.

Even so were she just walk away like that, though I were want her to stay. But she were only leave me with this strange notebook, go away, and not look back. And me feel so struck and never eat anything again.

Meanwhile I know I have to walk away too, and

head back into the town square. Where four sides do trap me, and the straight lines and angles seem be too strict in the morning sun. Were my mind very broke up, and me were run into a side street and take me down onto the town wharf. Because were me feel nerve trauma. Over the road, in the shade of a oak tree, were there this old wooden bench, where I were want to rest my head and close my eyes. Too wore out and tired were me just lay down and be a cat-cradle inbetween its two arms. Try and go to sleep in the morning cold. Only were I have this little blue notebook to read.

Were it very little, with the corners worn, and to my own cursive hand were the inscription on the front seem be so unmistakenly resemblant, *The Death of James Gray*. Open to the first page, it was a very unholy thing to see, were the italics too appear very thin and be my own. And there was nothing I can do.

THE
DEATH
OF
JAMES GRAY

WERE there once this poor starveling, who were a fall from grace and have to leave his only castle in the sky. Where he did study a lot, and learn of many great things. Though he were abandon everything he have ever known and just be a outcast now.

When once he was a scientist though, and some

modest understanding of nature he were very hungry to have. To seek explanation of naturally occurring phenomena was his only heartfelt desire. So were he spend all the time in that castle in the sky with his scientific studies and do pure researches. And in humankind were he see a truly progressive intellectual being, and too see promise in well meaning virtues and have forgiving ways. But were he have to look into his own heart and see his own simulate constructions were just a face and conceal his own innermost complacency. Then so a view of human well-being were just be arrogant and vain were he soon wake up to. Then it were plain to see how a responsible and creative souls were have their own native recklessness about them and be headstrong wilful. And in a world as this were scientific studies only ever provide unlimited technologies to careless peoples. With a progressive intellectual being be so disregarding were the consequences of experimental findings be very harmful. So were a lonely poor starveling just be very faithless now and forsake scientific endeavour for ever.

All the same were he remain indifferent to his scientific studies were only ever his own deliberate choosing, and just be his own intentional disregard. And in his heart were he know too how ignorance just be violence, and were they just be indistinguishable. Then were this intentional disregard of his only a most considered destructiveness. Except that to return to the research effort and resume in the furtherance of human knowledge were a bad thing to do. And do go in full circle. Again, only to heedless persons and remiss were he always provide scientific discovery.

And so, fallen in a impossible circle were James Gray just be helpless now. With no reason left and feel too distraught, all the time were he in torment in a lonely infidel starveling paradox. A paradox he so called, for to lost souls without promise were any favourable solution just be unworkable.

In that, 'were scientific endeavour effectuate harm from a ignorant and violent people, only to abandon scientific enquiry altogether were a most ignorant and violent action as well.'

Thoroughly insoluble were the sole outcome only ever be a utmost harm. To a lost soul with no belief it were this hopeless. Utterly faithless, James Gray were just burn in Hell.

And that was it! All it did ever say. And in my jeans' pocket were I quickly hide the tiny notebook away; were me not coming out of this one unscathed. And about me it did be so true!, most every word! And were I always keep in mind the useless destroying of my manuscript, and how in my dream were all human well-being just be presumptuous and vain.

Too long estranged were me just stare up at very blue skies and interminable. Where no birds do sing, and be so empty. Were my heart not know any real feeling. Do only be dissonance and damaged nerve tissue. For the remaining of my ever were I always have to see everything and life be runaway like water down the drain. And just be in hopelessness, and be so starless. With a very blue sky and morning seem be disquiet and unsettle though. With me in distraction were the sky have unwant about it and threaten me. And then do I see them! Fly heavenly high, so close in a ruthless summer sun. Too few Death Angels and just be bleeding.

AFTERWARDS

FOR when the night was through, and had I listened to his bleak and saddening tale, was all his laying bare to me his lonely frightened soul straight away the very first thing in my waking mind.

Though to me it seemed doubtful my friend would yet be wakeful, to see him missing from his bed was most remote and unexpected. With hurried surprise was I quick to my feet and out of the chair where I had drifted. So soon I was to make my way downstairs.

When in the kitchen was when the old man told me that my friend was gone away. With his elder understanding was he with sympathy in his saying of how he had disappeared so carelessly in the stone-cold of first matutinal shine, and were we not to deem him cruel for his living unconcerned and recklessly. For James was thoroughly heartbroken. Was he only too unwell and helpless that he had to leave without saying goodbye.

And so were all these affairs which happened to my friend just too unkind and so heartbreaking. Had he only set his life dreams against modern realities, which in retaliation were not very forgiving. So were there no a heaven-sent wish which would save him.

Watchful over the weakened old man were we only left in sorrowing, and in so a desolate way had I to leave him also. Further linger with my presence and offer cold comfort all that was left for me to do. And there the matter must rest.